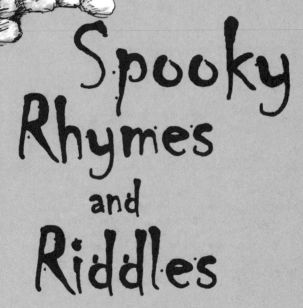

Spooky Rhymes and Riddles

by Lilian Moore
Pictures by Ib Ohlsson

SCHOLASTIC INC.

New York Toronto London Auckland Sydney
Mexico City New Delhi Hong Kong

To Ann McGovern Scheiner

ISBN 0-439-25974-6

Text copyright © 1972 by Lilian Moore.
Illustrations copyright © 1972 by Ib Ohlsson.
All rights reserved.
Published by Scholastic Inc.

12 11 10 9 8 7   2 3 4 5/0

Printed in the U.S.A.   23

First Scholastic printing, October 2000

The Ghost
in Our Apartment House

The ghost
in our apartment house
makes everybody late.
He gets into the elevator,
closes the gate,
presses all the buttons
from one to eight,
rides up and down and
up and down
while all the people wait.

The Monster's Pet

What kind of pet
Would a monster get
If a monster set
His mind on a pet?

Would it snuffle and wuffle
Or snackle and snore?
Would it slither and dither
Or rattle and roar?

Would it dribble and bribble
In manner horr-rible
Or squibble and squirm
Like a worm?

And every day
In pleasant weather,
Would they go out
For a walk together?

When a Monster Scolds Her Children

When a monster scolds her children
Does she say,
"I'm not very pleased with you.
You weren't MEAN today!
Monster Daddy will be sad
When he hears you weren't BAD!"

Ghost Baby

Mama Ghost and Baby Ghost
Played a game of peek-a-boo.
Baby Ghost looked up and cried,
"I see through you!
I see through you!"

What to Say to an Alligator

If a smiling alligator
With his jaws open wide,
Says, "Tummy tum tum,
Dear child, come inside!"

Just say
"Yummy yum yum,
I really can't come.
Instead of me,
Try bubble gum!"

The Friendly Guy

I'm a very friendly
guy
I always say,
"Oh hi!"

I greet the people that I meet
But I don't understand —
No one I meet on any street
Wants to shake my hand.

No one will
try.
I can't think
why.

What was
howling
and yowling
all night long?
Did you say cat?
Wrong!

It was the wind.

It wraps you
in its ghostly arms,
a gray and clammy thing.
Yet if you move
it lets you go
and never says a thing!

Fog

The Ghost Goes to the Supermarket

Whang! go the soup cans.
Thump! the potatoes.
Slurp! goes the syrup.
Squish! the tomatoes.

The soda pop slops.
The popcorn scrunches.
The jelly beans bounce.
The sugar crunches.

"I'm just looking for the toast,"
Says the ghost.

Mrs. O'Gray

Mrs. O'Gray
hung her wash out one day.
What a surprise!

In front of her eyes
a sheet went a-flapping,
a-twirling and snapping.
It moaned and it groaned
and away it flew.

Why it did that
she never knew.

Greedy Goblin

Once there was a goblin,
a greedy greedy goblin,
who ran around a-gobblin' up
everyone he met.
A goblin
a-gobblin'
whomever he could get.

The greedy greedy goblin
grew fat
from head to feet,
which happens when you gobble up
everyone you meet.

He has to go a-wobblin' now.
He can't run 'round a-gobblin' now.
And for a greedy goblin, how
hard to go a-wobblin'
to catch someone to eat!

Listen!

Listen to the witch!

grinch grinch grunch

chip-chop crunch

grickle grackle grooble grobble

munch munch munch

Whatever in the world
is she having for lunch?

Cat

Cat,
Cat,
Your eyes are bright and green.
Where have you been
What have you done
So skittery-scary this Hallowe'en?

And where did you get
that pointed hat?
Tell me *that*,
Cat!

Spooky Riddles

What has one horn
And doesn't need more,
Because people run
When it comes with a roar?

A truck

What's the hair-iest
scari-est
thing
you could see
on your street?

A gorilla

What's even
hair-ier
scari-er?

Two gorillas!

IT'S
Right behind you,
Creeps on the ground,
Follows you home,
Does not make a sound.

Better turn 'round —

Your shadow!

"Look at you,"
The old witch said.
"You're no use to me
Till I cut off your head!"

(The witch is talking to a head
of cabbage in the garden.)

The Monster's Birthday

Oh, what a party!
They all ate hearty
   of elegant bellyache stew.

Then came the cake
In the shape of a snake
   and trimmed with octopus goo.

The balloons all went BANG!
And everyone sang,
   "Happy Birthday, dear Monster, to you."

Johnny Drew a Monster

Johnny drew a monster.
The monster chased him.
Just in time
Johnny erased him.

There Was an Egg

There was an egg that grew and grew.
What was inside? No one knew.

It grew and grew, big as a hat,
Big as a house, and bigger than that.

Oh what a CRACK was heard one day!
People screamed and ran away.

They tiptoed back and found the shell.
What hatched out? They couldn't tell!

And no one knows.
Do you suppose....

Something Is There

Something is there

      there on the stair,

           coming down

               coming down

                  stepping with care.

                     Coming down

                        coming down

                           slinkety-sly.

Something is coming and wants to get by.

Spooky Limericks

There once was a three-headed shmoo
Who said, "I'd rather have two.
  It's not all this brain
  That gives me a pain.
It's the tipping of hats I must do!"

There once was a thirsty gorilla
Who wanted to drink sarsaparilla
  He bought up a vat full
  And filled up a hat full
And oops! Sarsaparilla did spilla!

Said the Witch, "I like riding high
And looping-the-loop in the sky.
　　But lately, good heavens,
　　Those seven-forty-sevens
Make it quite tricky to try!"

A Dragon whose size was quite whopping
Breathed fire all day without stopping.
　　No child seemed to mind
　　For he really was kind
And kept all the popcorn a-popping.

Poem about THEM

THEY
   polish their broomsticks,
   sharpen their hats,
   catch some spiders,
   feed the bats,
   try out some yowls
   with all the cats.
THEN
   witches are ready for
YOU
   KNOW
      WHEN!

When a Ghost Gets Smudgy

When a ghost gets smudgy and it's Hallowe'en
Does he hop into a washing machine
where he
  swooshes and swishes
  and splashes and sloshes
  and spins-es and rinses
and comes out clean?

The Witch's Song

Hey! Cackle! Hey!
Let's have fun today.
    All shoelaces will have knots.
    No knots will untie.
    Every glass of milk will spill.
    Nothing wet will dry.
    Every pencil point will break.
    And everywhere in town
    Peanut-buttered bread will drop
    Upside down!
Hey! Hey! Hey!
Have a pleasant day!

Bedtime Story

"Tell me a story," says Witch's Child.
"About the Beast so fierce and wild.
About a Ghost that shrieks and groans,
A skeleton that rattles bones,
About a Monster, crawly-creepy.
Something nice to make me sleepy."

Teeny Tiny Ghost

A teeny tiny ghost
no bigger than a mouse,
at most,
lived in a great big house.

It's hard to haunt
a great big house
when you're a teeny tiny ghost
no bigger than a mouse,
at most.

He did what he could do.

So every dark and stormy night —
the kind that shakes a house with fright —
if you stood still and listened right,
you'd hear a
teeny
tiny

BOO!